THE NOTEBOOK OF DOOM

CHARGE OF THE LIGHTNING BUGS

by Troy Cummings

BRANCHES

SCHOLASTIC INC.

TABLE OF CONTENTS

To Nate: The smartest, funniest brother ever. Also: Banana banana banana!

Thank you, Katie Carella and Liz Herzog, for your high-energy editing and positively-charged art direction.

No part of this publication may be reproduced, stored in a retrieval system, or transmitted in any form or by any means, electronic, mechanical, photocopying, recording, or otherwise, without written permission of the publisher. For information regarding permission, write to Scholastic Inc., Attention: Permissions Department, 557 Broadway, New York, NY 10012.

Library of Congress Cataloging-in-Publication Data

Cummings, Troy, author.
Charge of the lightning bugs / by Troy Cummings.
pages cm. – (The Notebook of Doom ; 8)
Summary: It is the first day of the brand-new Stermont Elementary School, but everything electrical seems to be going haywire, and it looks like strange green lightning bugs are draining off the power–but when they see green lightning in a clear blue sky Alexander and his friends know there must be a monster involved.
ISBN 0-545-79555-9 (pbk.) – ISBN 0-545-79554-0 (hardcover) – ISBN 0-545-79556-7 (ebook) – ISBN 0-545-79557-5 (eba ebook) 1. Monsters–Juvenile fiction. 2. Fireflies–Juvenile fiction. 3. Elementary schools–Juvenile fiction. 4. Friendship–Juvenile fiction. 5. Horror tales. [1. Monsters–Fiction. 2. Fireflies–Fiction. 3. Schools–Fiction. 4. Friendship–Fiction. 5. Horror stories.] I. Title. II. Series: Cummings, Troy. Notebook of doom ; 8.
PZ7.C91494Cf 2015
813.6–dc23
[Fic]
2014048234

ISBN 978-0-545-79554-8 (hardcover)/ISBN 978-0-545-79555-5 (paperback)

10 9 8 7 6 5 4 3 2 1   15 16 17 18 19/0

Printed in China   38
First Scholastic printing, July 2015

Book design by Liz Herzog

1 TWENTY QUESTIONS

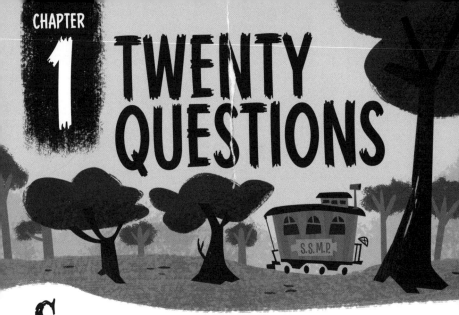

School hadn't started yet, but Alexander was about to take a quiz. It wasn't a math quiz or a spelling quiz. It was a super-secret quiz about monsters. His two best friends, Rip and Nikki, had made it for him.

Alexander grabbed his pencil and got to work.

> **Super-secret MONSTER QUIZ!**
>
> NAME: _Alexander Bopp_   NICKNAME: _Salamander_
>
> SHOE SIZE: $4\frac{1}{2}$
>
> BIRTHDAY: _February 29_
>
> FAVORITE SOUP: _Chicken noodle_
>
> 1. Balloon goons suck air. (True)/ False
>
> 2. Draw a jampire.
>
> A GOOD monster. (Hi, Nikki!)
>
> Sees in the dark.
>
> Eats red juicy stuff.
>
> Avoids sunlight.

He raced through the questions. *True! False! All of the above! Don't get eaten!* The quiz was totally easy, until he got to question #20.

> 20. What's the stinkiest monster in the notebook?
>
> ~~sewer slug~~   ~~cheese-blaster~~
>
> saber-toothed skunk?

DING! Rip hit a bell. "Time's up, weenie!"

"Let's see how you did!" said Nikki.

Rip, Nikki, and Alexander were the three members of the Super Secret Monster Patrol. They were hanging out in an old caboose in the woods: S.S.M.P. headquarters.

Alexander handed his quiz to Nikki.

"Nice work, Salamander," she said. "You're a grade-A monster-fighter. Or grade-A-minus, anyhow. You missed the last question."

"Nuts," said Alexander. "So, which monster *is* the stinkiest?"

Nikki held up an old notebook. It said S.S.M.P. on the cover, and its pages were full of monster drawings. She flipped it open and passed it to Alexander.

TRASH-SQUATCH

Walking heap of garbage.

HABITAT Out at the curb, every Tuesday.

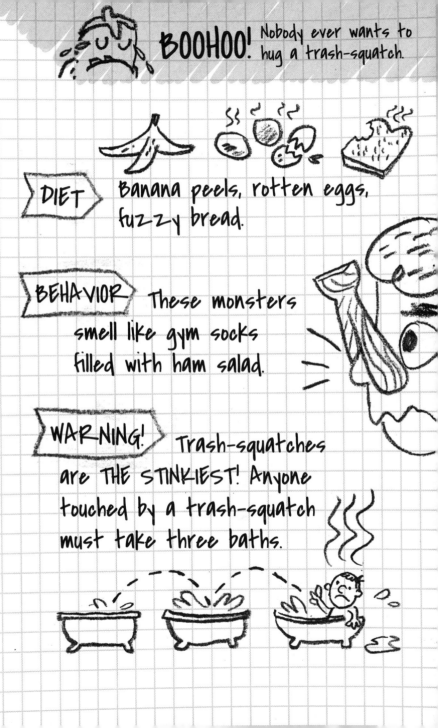

BOOHOO! Nobody ever wants to hug a trash-squatch.

DIET Banana peels, rotten eggs, fuzzy bread.

BEHAVIOR These monsters smell like gym socks filled with ham salad.

WARNING! Trash-squatches are THE STINKIEST! Anyone touched by a trash-squatch must take three baths.

"Of course!" said Alexander as he snapped the notebook shut. "Nothing stinks worse than a trash-squatch!"

"Except for the end of summer vacation," said Rip. "I cannot believe we're going back to school tomorrow."

"Speak for yourself," said Nikki. "I can't *wait* for school to start. We'll be in a brand-new building! With a brand-new teacher!"

"I guess so," said Rip. "And I *will* be able to show off my awesome new shoes. They light up when I walk!"

"HEY, KIDDO!" sang a far-off voice. "DINNERTIME!"

"That's my dad," said Alexander, tossing the notebook in his backpack. "Gotta go! See you tomorrow!"

CHAPTER 2
AN ALARMING GIFT

Alexander followed the smell of sizzling steak to his backyard. His dad was standing near the grill.

"Hi, Al!" he said, waving a spatula. "Welcome to our last cookout of the summer!"

Alexander took a seat at the picnic table. They ate steak-and-cheese sandwiches as the sun went down.

"And now," said his dad, "here's a little back-to-school surprise!"

He gave Alexander a gift. "Thanks, dad!" said Alexander. He ripped off the wrapping paper.

"An alarm clock," said Alexander. "*Uh*, just what I needed."

"I know!" said his dad, smiling. "You're always running late, so I thought—" His dad paused. "What's that? Over by the woods?"

A tiny green spark flashed at the edge of the yard. A moment later, some more sparks began zigzagging through the air.

"Well, rinse my molars!" Alexander's dad said. "Lightning bugs! It's awfully late in the year for them!" He got up and headed toward the house. "I'll be right back, Al!"

Alexander watched the glowing bugs drift across his backyard. There were now hundreds of them. He felt like an astronaut in a galaxy of tiny green stars.

Alexander's dad came back out, carrying an empty jar.

"Let's catch some lightning bugs!" he said.

Alexander looked at the jar. "Will they be okay in there?" he asked.

"Sure!" said his dad. "I poked holes in the lid. They'll be fine!"

Alexander and his dad ran around the yard, snatching lighting bugs. Before long, the jar was glowing like a lantern.

"Perfect," said Alexander's dad. "Now, off to bed! I'll come tuck you in after I clean up."

Alexander carried the glowing jar into his bedroom. He put on his pajamas, brushed his teeth, and plopped into bed.

A minute later, Alexander's dad came in, carrying the new alarm clock.

"You left this outside!" he said. He put the clock on the nightstand and pressed a few buttons. "There. Your alarm is set for 6:30 A.M. That should give us plenty of time for a nice, fresh start."

Alexander's dad turned out the light and closed the door. The bugs glowed green, but a little dimmer than before.

Alexander tapped on the jar. "Poor little guys," he said.

He got out of bed and opened his window. Then he unscrewed the lid on the jar.

"You're free," he whispered. "Now shoo!"

The lightning bugs flew out of the jar. But they didn't leave his room. One landed on his alarm clock, glowing extra bright.

"Good night, bugs," said Alexander, climbing back into bed.

He watched the twinkling bugs swirl around his ceiling until he fell asleep.

3 ZERO O'CLOCK

The next morning, Alexander woke up feeling groggy. The lightning bugs were all gone. He yawned as he glanced over at his new alarm clock.

Alexander rubbed his eyes. *Zero o'clock?* he thought. *That's impossible!*

The clock's screen blinked. Then it displayed a strange symbol.

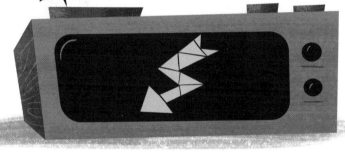

Alexander sat up. *Huh?*

The clock's screen went dim.

Alexander hit a few buttons, but the clock stayed dark.

Great, he thought. *My brand-new alarm clock is already broken. What time is it?*

He got up, and shuffled out of his bedroom. He could hear his dad snoring.

There was a grandfather clock in the hallway.

Little hand points halfway between 10 and 11.

It doesn't really matter where the big hand is pointing. Alexander is late!

"DAD! Wake up!" Alexander screamed. "We overslept!"

THUNK! Alexander's dad fell out of bed. He staggered into the hallway.

"Hey, Al," he said. He yawned wide, like a lion. "My alarm clock seems to be dead."

"Yours, too?" said Alexander. "That's —"

"Holy overbite!" shouted Alexander's dad, pointing to the grandfather clock. "It's after ten thirty! We overslept! We have to go NOW!"

Alexander raced to his room to get dressed. He dashed downstairs. His dad was already there, brushing his teeth in the kitchen sink.

"Grab a banana for breakfast, Al!" he said. "And you'll have to buy lunch today!" He ran to the door. "Meet me at the car. Go, go, go!"

Alexander tried to tie his shoes with one hand and eat a banana with the other. Then he headed outside.

His dad ran over to him, wearing a helmet.

"Change of plans!" he yelled. "We're taking our bikes! The car won't start — the battery must be dead!"

"That's too bad," said Alexander.

They jumped on their bikes and pedaled down the driveway.

"Good luck, kiddo!" said Alexander's dad.

"See you after school!" said Alexander.

They rode off in opposite directions.

CHAPTER 4

FALLING UP

Alexander coasted to a stop at a shiny, new bike rack near his shiny, new school.

Windmill
Uses wind to make electricity.

Dome on top
What's it for?

Greenhouse
For growing plants.

Solar panels
Use sunlight to make electricity.

Top part
Metal and glass, like a skyscraper.

Bottom part
Made of stone, like a castle.

STERMONT
ELEMENTARY

Alexander ran inside. The lobby was fourteen stories tall, with fourteen-story windows letting in fourteen-stories' worth of sunlight. The back wall was lined with escalators.

There was a desk in the middle of the lobby. Alexander read the nameplate on the desk.

MR. HOARSELY
SECRETARY
(Also: Bus driver. Nurse. Gym teacher. Janitor.)

Alexander did not see anyone, so he rang the bell.

"Eep!" Mr. Hoarsely jumped up from beneath the desk.

"Why were you hiding?" asked Alexander.

Mr. Hoarsely pointed to the ceiling. "Because I have to sit under *this*!" he said.

Alexander looked up. A huge sculpture hung over the desk, sort of like a mobile hanging over a crib. Except instead of little clouds and rainbows, this mobile was a bunch of spiky cement balls.

Alexander frowned. "That sculpture is more ugly than scary," he said.

Mr. Hoarsely gulped, loudly. It was hard to believe that he was once a member of the S.S.M.P.

"So, anyway," said Alexander, "can you tell me where my classroom is?"

Mr. Hoarsely checked the time. His eyebrows shot up. "Oh, my! You're so, so late! It's almost lunchtime!" He grabbed his clipboard. "Let's see, sixth graders are on the ground floor . . . kindergarteners are on the eleventh floor. And the thirteenth floor is off limits, of course. *Ah!* Here you are — ninth floor! Dr. Tallow's class."

CLICK! The desk lamp suddenly switched off.

Mr. Hoarsely gave Alexander a worried look. He turned the lamp back on.

"Okay, thanks!" said Alexander. He ran to the escalator, but stopped at the bottom. The metal steps were whirring up fast. *Too* fast!

He counted to three and jumped on.

ZWOOP! The escalator whisked Alexander to the second floor. He felt like a character in a video game.

He hopped onto the next escalator. It was moving even faster. He heard the wind whoosh by his ears until — **FLUMP!** — he was thrown off on the third floor.

Alexander sat up, blinking.

Whoa, he thought. *I don't remember escalators being so speedy!*

He still had six floors to go.

SHOCKINGLY LATE

Alexander had almost gotten the hang of the super-fast escalators by the time he made it to the ninth floor.

He scooted down the carpeted hallway to a big yellow door.

NO RUNNING!

Dr. Tallow's Class

Alexander pulled the door handle.

A jolt of electricity shocked his hand. **AAACK!** He yelped as the door swung open.

Everyone in the room looked up from their school books. Rip and Nikki waved from the back row. Actually, Nikki waved. Rip crossed his eyes and stuck out his tongue.

"*Uh,*" said Alexander, tugging his backpack straps. "The door zapped me."

Alexander's new teacher was writing on the board.

She capped her marker and turned around.

"Sorry I'm late," Alexander mumbled.

STAR SHOW TOMORROW

Dr. Tallow grinned so wide, it stretched out her face.

"No worries, sweetie," she said. "It's only the first day of school." She spoke warmly, like someone lulling a puppy to sleep.

Alexander took a step into the room. It was cheery and warm — nothing like his old classroom in the broken-down hospital.

Windows!

Posters!

Bookcases!

New desks!

Odd door...

STAR SHOW TOMORROW

Dr. Tallow led Alexander to a desk in the front row. Then she went back to the board. "Tomorrow," she said, "we'll see a Star Show in our planetarium."

The ceiling lights began to flicker.

"Not again!" groaned Rip.

Alexander looked up at the lights. He could hear a faint humming sound.

Dr. Tallow kept smiling. "Don't worry! If the lights go out, we have these sunny windows." She glanced at the clock. "But since the lights *are* acting up, why don't you head down to the second floor? We'll start lunch early."

Everyone cheered for their new teacher. Except Nikki. She yanked her hoodie down over her face. All Alexander could see was her frown.

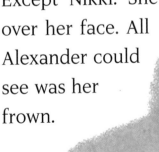

6 DOWNWARD MARCH!

"**S**alamander, you're the most late-to-school kid in history," said Rip, on their way to lunch.

"I overslept," said Alexander. "I'm just glad Dr. Tallow wasn't mad. She seems great!"

"Yeah, I guess," said Nikki.

"Come on, slowpokes!" said Rip.

They rushed toward the escalators.

"Last one to the cafeteria is a trash-squatch! Huh?!" Rip stopped in his tracks.

The escalators were no longer running at super speed. In fact, they weren't running at all.

"Uh-oh," said Nikki. "Looks like we're *walking* down to lunch."

CLOMP! CLOMP! They joined the rest of their classmates in the long march down to lunch. Rip's new shoes lit up with each step.

They passed a tired-looking teacher huffing and puffing up the opposite escalator. He was carrying a big bunch of pens.

"Hi, Mr. Plunkett!" said Alexander. "What's with all the pens?"

"Oh, hi, students," he said. "Our electric pencil sharpeners are on the fritz! My class needs *something* to write with."

Mr. Plunkett trudged up to the next floor.

That's strange, thought Alexander. *I saw Mr. Hoarsely's lamp flick off, too — all by itself.*

Alexander, Rip, and Nikki finally reached the shiny new lunchroom on the second floor.

"Look!" said Nikki, pointing to an electronic screen on the wall. "A normal lunch, for once!"

"Yes!" Rip shouted. He high-fived Alexander.

The friends were jolted back by a quick, painful shock.

"Ow!" said Alexander. "Why do I keep getting shocked today?"

"Are you dragging your feet on the new carpet?" said Nikki. "Sometimes that can make you get zapped."

BZZZT!

Then the menu screen flickered, and the words changed.

"You guys," Alexander whispered, "I think that message is a warning! For us!"

Nikki scrunched up her face. "What are you getting at, Salamander?"

Alexander yanked the notebook from his backpack. "What if there's an *invisible* monster in our school?!" he said. "Maybe *it* wrote the message!"

He flipped the notebook open.

MANTA X-RAY

Invisible floating flat fish

HABITAT Any hard-to-reach place. (Behind the television, the top shelf of the bookcase, under the refrigerator.)

SPLORP! Manta x-ray slime is good for oiling a bike chain.

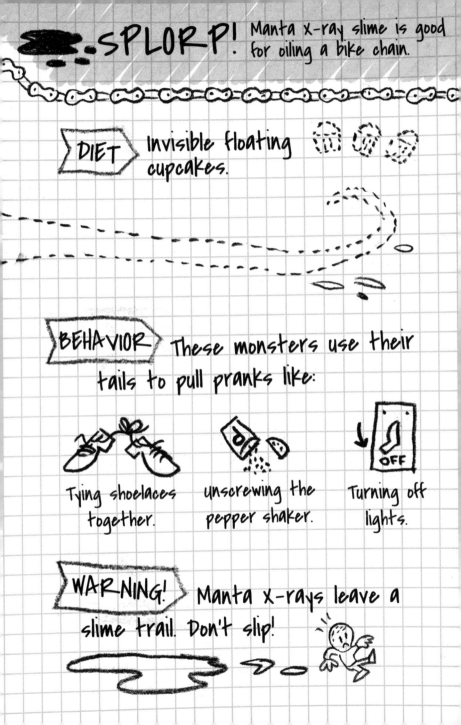

> **DIET** Invisible floating cupcakes.

> **BEHAVIOR** These monsters use their tails to pull pranks like:

Tying shoelaces together.

unscrewing the pepper shaker.

Turning off lights.

> **WARNING!** Manta x-rays leave a slime trail. Don't slip!

CHAPTER 7

WALKIE-TALKIE SHOUTIE

TODAY'S MENU

YOU'D BETTER NOT **BUG** US. OR ELSE!

lexander closed the notebook.

"There's no manta x-ray," said Rip. "We'd see slime everywhere."

"Good point," said Alexander. "But there is definitely *something* weird going on." He squinted up at the menu. "That clearly looks like a warning to me. And what does that jagged arrow mean? I feel like I've seen it before . . ."

"Maybe the cafeteria workers haven't figured out the new menu," said Nikki. "Grown-ups always have trouble with computers."

BZZZT! A second later, the screen changed back. Sort of.

TODAY'S MENU

Cheesy banana shrimp-loaf

Pickles & cream

Garlic sherbert

"Noooo!" Rip shouted at the screen. "Go back to *snickerdoodles!*"

The three friends got their trays and took a seat. Alexander used his fork to draw a zigzag arrow on his cheesy banana shrimp-loaf.

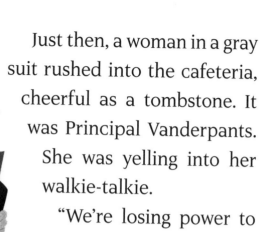

Just then, a woman in a gray suit rushed into the cafeteria, cheerful as a tombstone. It was Principal Vanderpants. She was yelling into her walkie-talkie.

"We're losing power to the lights, the escalators, and the snack machines! You're the electrician — fix the electricity!"

The voice on the other end sounded scared. "Yes, ma'am. I'm on the roof. Your power levels are down to three percent. But, *uh*, I'm not sure where the electricity is going."

"Well, figure it out!" said Ms. Vanderpants. "The Star Show is tomorrow, and it had better go off without a hitch!"

She marched out of earshot.

"Wow, did you hear that?" asked Alexander.

"Yeah!" said Rip. "Our new school has snack machines!"

"No, shrimp-loaf!" said Nikki. "The part about the school having electrical problems."

Alexander pushed his tray aside. "It's not just the *school* that's having problems," he said. "This morning, my dad's car battery died. And before that, my alarm clock stopped working." His jaw dropped. "My clock! It flashed the same jagged arrow as the lunch menu!"

"*Hmmm . . .*" said Nikki. "I guess that arrow *could* be a warning."

"Big deal," said Rip. "I got five warnings per day in kindergarten."

The three friends returned their trays and began the long walk up to class.

Oh, my word!" said Dr. Tallow as her students slumped into their seats. "You are all out of breath!"

"No kidding," said Rip. "We just climbed up seven flights of broken escalators!"

Dr. Tallow walked to the odd door at the back of the room. The door had a keypad instead of a handle. "Well, then," she said, "perhaps it's time for a treat!" She punched in a code, and the door swung open. "Follow me!"

The students looked at one another. Then they followed her inside.

"Welcome to our brand-new, state-of-the-art classroom-pet zone," said Dr. Tallow. "This is where we'll learn all about these incredible animals!"

The room was bright and clean with cages along the walls. The cages held every kind of classroom pet.

The students perked right up.

"Today's lesson is about cocoons," Dr. Tallow said. "Cocoons protect certain kinds of insects as they grow. Can anyone name an insect that makes a cocoon?"

"Easy!" said Nikki. "A butterfly!"

"*Ooh*, sorry. Not quite," said Dr. Tallow. "A butterfly comes from a *chrysalis*. A moth comes from a cocoon."

Nikki frowned at her teacher.

Dr. Tallow waved everyone over to a small glass case.

"Look closely," said Dr. Tallow. "See if you can find a cocoon in here."

Alexander spotted the cocoon right away, under a leaf.

But before he could point it out — **BZZZT!** The room went dark. Students gasped.

A moment later, a red light on the ceiling began flashing. It made strange shadows under Dr. Tallow's eyes.

"That's the safety light," she said. "It comes on when there's a power outage."

The regular lights flickered back on, followed by a buzzing sound from the intercom.

STUDENTS! This is Principal Vanderpants. We're having power problems, so class is canceled. You will have recess outside for the rest of the day.

The students cheered. Alexander watched a hermit crab tuck itself back into its shell.

"To make up for today's missed classes," continued Ms. Vanderpants, "you will have no recess for the next two weeks."

The cheering stopped. The crab came back out of its shell.

CHAPTER 9 DON'T WALK

The all-afternoon recess seemed to fly by on shiny new swings, slides, and monkey bars. Alexander, Rip, and Nikki walked away from the playground happy and tired.

"Look," said Nikki. She pointed to the school. "Now the whole building is dark!"

Rip grinned. "Maybe no power means ALL-DAY recess tomorrow!"

44

"I don't get it," said Alexander as he unlocked his bike. "Our school has a wind fan and solar panels! It should be powering itself!"

They walked a few blocks, and stopped at a busy intersection. Honking cars were backed up in all directions.

"Whoa!" said Nikki. "Major traffic jam!"

"All these cars are waiting for a green light," Rip said, looking up at the stoplight.

Alexander followed Rip's gaze. The stoplight was dark.

Alexander shook his head. "Let's cross the street and get out of here."

They looked at the crossing signal. It showed a red *stop* hand for a few seconds, and then it switched to a green *walk* figure.

But then — **BZZZT!**

The *walk* figure became a skeleton!

"A skeleton?!" said Rip. "How'd *that* get up there?!"

The signal flashed again. The skeleton was replaced by a zigzag arrow.

"Look!" said Alexander. "The same shape from my clock and the menu!"

"Another warning?" said Nikki. "Is *everything* in town going wonky?"

"Well, everything that uses electricity," said Alexander.

"You were right, Salamander. This must be the work of a monster!" said Rip. "Is there a machines-act-weird monster in the notebook?"

"*Hmm,*" said Alexander. He leaned his bike against a mailbox and pulled out the notebook. "Maybe a rust-buster?"

RUST-BUSTER
Metal-eating monster.

HABITAT Shipyards, iron mines, used-car lots.

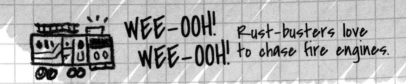
WEE-OOH! WEE-OOH! Rust-busters love to chase fire engines.

> **DIET** Dishwashers, bulldozers, lawn mowers ... Any kind of metal machine.

> **BEHAVIOR** These monsters breathe a cloud of mist that causes metal to instantly rust.

Mmmm! Cinnamon!

> **WARNING!** Rust-busters are allergic to wood. Hide in a tree house to be safe.

"That can't be right," said Nikki. "Machines aren't being eaten. They're just losing power."

BRINGGGG!

Alexander's dad coasted up on his bike.

"Hey, kiddos! Traffic's a nightmare!" he said. "Good thing we didn't take the car today."

"Yeah," said Alexander.

"You know," Alexander's dad went on, "this whole day has been bonkers. My dental chairs kept folding up on people! And I called every electrician in town, but they were all busy."

Alexander looked at Rip and Nikki.

"Well, hurry home, Al," said Alexander's dad. **BRINGGG! BRRINNGG!** His dad biked off.

Alexander strapped on his helmet. "Keep an eye on your lights and clocks and stuff," he whispered to Rip and Nikki.

A glowing green bug flew past Nikki's nose.

"A lightning bug!" said Nikki.

"They were all over my yard last night," said Alexander.

"But in the daytime?" asked Rip. "Weird."

The three friends watched the lightning bug land on the crosswalk signal. The zigzag arrow blinked, and then went dark.

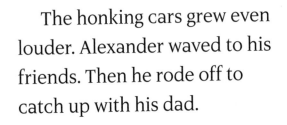

The honking cars grew even louder. Alexander waved to his friends. Then he rode off to catch up with his dad.

CHAPTER 10 GREEN LIGHTNING

The next morning, everything seemed to be back-to-normal.

Alexander met Rip and Nikki in the school lobby. The lights were working, the escalators were working, and Mr. Hoarsely was working.

"Maybe we were wrong, guys," said Nikki, as they rode up the escalator.

"Yeah," said Rip. "Maybe the screwy stuff yesterday was just plain old electric problems."

"You're right," said Alexander. "Everything *seems* normal. But how could stuff all over town just fix itself overnight? And besides, what about those messages we saw? A monster must be to blame!"

Rip and Nikki shrugged as they headed into class.

"Hello, dearies," said Dr. Tallow. "Take your seats."

As Alexander sat down, he heard a rumble of thunder.

Everyone turned to look outside. The sky was perfectly blue. And cloudless.

Then — **FLASH!** — a streak of green lightning filled the sky. The students sat up straighter.

Green lightning? thought Alexander.

"Well, that's odd," said Dr. Tallow.

There was another flash. The boy next to Alexander jumped.

"There, there," said Dr. Tallow. "Don't be scared." She opened a cabinet and pulled out a poster. "I'll teach you how to stay safe from lightning."

She tacked the poster to the wall.

LIGHTNING IS FRIGHTENING!

STAY INDOORS
when you see lightning!

HEAD FOR SHELTER
when you hear thunder!

NEVER TAKE A BATH
during a thunderstorm!

Take it from me,
Linda the Lightning Rod!

"What's a lightning rod?" Alexander asked.

"It's a metal pole that attracts lightning," said Dr. Tallow. "Benjamin Franklin invented it! Lightning strikes the rod instead of striking the house. Then the electricity flows safely through the rod, down to the ground."

BRUGHHMMMM! There was another rumble of thunder. But still, no clouds.

"Lightning rods protect houses. But do you know what can protect *you* from electricity?" Dr. Tallow continued. "Rubber! Here, feel it!"

She passed around a pair of rubber gloves. "Rubber blocks the flow of electricity."

"Maybe they should just build rubber houses," said Rip as green lightning filled the sky.

BZZZT! The lights in the room flickered.

Dr. Tallow looked at the clock. "Let's head up to the planetarium. I really want you to see the Star Show, and I'm worried we may have more electrical problems heading our way."

More electrical problems? thought Alexander. He looked around. Then he stuffed the rubber gloves into his backpack.

CHAPTER 11
WRITTEN IN THE STARS

The big lights overhead kept flickering as Alexander's class headed into the hall.

"Huh?!" said Rip, stopping at the escalators.

The escalators were running, but they were all going down.

One by one, the students leaped onto the escalator, and ran up as fast as they could against the falling steps.

"It's like ... a treadmill," said Nikki, between breaths.

"This star show . . ." said Rip, " . . . had better be . . . awesome."

"No . . . kidding," Alexander huffed.

Finally, the panting students finished their climb. They were in a glass-walled room full of plants: the greenhouse.

"Hey!" said Nikki. "This is where we fought the veggie monsters!"

Alexander hunched over, gasping for breath. He was seeing stars! *No, wait.* Another *lightning bug?* He reached out to catch it and — **BZZZT!** — a tiny spark shot out, jolting his hand.

"OW!" Alexander yelped. "Did you see that?!"

"Huh?" said Rip.

"I just got zapped by that lightning bug!" said Alexander. He looked around, but the bug had flown off.

"Very funny, weenie," said Rip. "Lightning bugs don't zap people."

"Maybe not *regular* lightning bugs," said Alexander.

"Come on, guys," said Nikki. "The planetarium is this way."

PLANETARIUM

They followed their classmates up a twisty staircase. It led to a bubble-shaped room with recliner chairs along the walls.

"Oh!" said Rip. "We're inside that little dome on top of our school!"

Mr. Hoarsely sat at the control panel, turning knobs and pressing buttons.

"Welcome to the Star Show," he said. "Have a seat. And don't be scared, even if it gets really"— he gulped — "dark!"

The lights dimmed. And hundreds of stars covered the ceiling.

"*Oooooh!*" said everyone. They all stargazed in silence.

But then, with a low hum, the stars began to move. They danced across the ceiling, forming pictures — like a giant dot-to-dot puzzle.

"A winged horse!" said Nikki.

"A crab!" said Rip.

"A bear!" said Alexander. He leaned over to Mr. Hoarsely. "These stars are so cool!"

"But I haven't turned on the star machine yet!" said Mr. Hoarsely, flipping switches.

BZZZT! The stars flickered, and began glowing neon green.

"Huh?!" said Rip.

"*Green* stars?!" whispered Nikki.

Alexander sat bolt upright. "They're not stars!" he said. "They're lightning bugs!"

"Those guys really get around!" said Rip.

The bugs flew every-which-way. Then they came together to spell a message.

"Those bugs . . ." said Nikki, "they must be monsters!"

The bugs vanished. The room went dark.

CHAPTER 12 A BRIGHT IDEA

Alexander could hear the screams of freaked-out students (and Mr. Hoarsely) running around the pitch-black planetarium.

"Nikki!" Alexander shouted. "What can you see with your night vision?"

"Everyone is scrambling to find the exit!" she said.

"We've got to get the other students out of here," said Alexander. "But it's too dark!"

"You need light, weenie?" said Rip. "Stand back. It's *my* time to shine!"

Rip stamped his foot. His shoe made a flash of light.

"Rip, you're a genius!" said Alexander. "Keep doing that!"

Rip stomped in place, lighting up the room every couple of seconds.

"Everyone!" Alexander yelled. "Walk toward Rip's shoe lights! He's near the exit! Then Mr. Hoarsely will lead you back to class!"

Mr. Hoarsely peeked out from his hiding spot. "I *will*?" he said. "Oh, right! I will! Follow me!" He led the other students out of the planetarium.

"What about us?" asked Nikki.

Rip was still stomping, but a little slower now. "Yeah! Aren't we going downstairs, too?"

"Nope. We're going upstairs — to the roof!" said Alexander. He pointed to a nearby ladder. It led up to a hatch in the ceiling.

Rip stopped stomping. The room went back to being dark.

"Are you nuts?!" said Rip. "That warning said to stay *off* the roof!"

"And don't forget about the lightning!" said Nikki. "We should not be up there when it's lightning out!"

"But it's not *real* lightning!" said Alexander. "*Monsters* are behind this! We've got to get up there and stop them!"

BZZZT! The lightning bugs suddenly lit up the dome above their heads. Now the bugs were glowing all kinds of colors: pink, purple, yellow, green, and blue.

The bugs swirled around, and then lined up in a pointy zigzag formation.

"Hey! There's that jagged arrow again!" said Alexander. "But wait, it's not an arrow. It's a lightning bolt!"

The lightning-bolt shape floated in place for a moment. Then it zoomed straight at Alexander's head.

13 BZZZT! ZAP! OW!

"Yipes!" Alexander dove behind a row of seats. The swarm of lightning bugs just missed him. The bugs smashed into the control panel. The planetarium lit up like a disco.

The bugs spun around in a dizzy whirl. Then they darted toward Alexander, Rip, and Nikki.

"Watch out, guys!" shouted Alexander. "Their zaps hurt!"

BZZZT! A pink bug zapped Rip's ear. "*Ow!* You weren't kidding!"

BZZZT! A blue bug zapped Nikki's hand. "*Ack!*"

BZZZT! A yellow one zapped Alexander on the nose. "Cut it out!"

The three friends waved and danced and flailed their arms like string puppets.

"Quick!" Alexander yelled. "To the roof!"

They scrambled up the ladder, surrounded by a cloud of angry, zapping bugs.

CLACK! They popped out of the hatch. The air on the roof felt dry and crackly. Green forks of lightning ripped through the sky.

BZZZT! "Ouch!" yelled Rip. He swatted a bug, knocking it to the ground. He smiled, and lifted his foot above the bug. "Squishy-time!" he said, stomping down hard.

His shoe flashed. But the bug had zipped out of the way. It hovered near his shoe and started humming loudly.

The rest of the bugs froze in midair.

"What's happening?" asked Alexander.

At once, all of the lightning bugs started buzzing around Rip.

"Get away!" Rip shouted. He danced an angry jig, but the bugs stuck to his blinking shoes.

Then the bugs flew up high and out of sight.

Rip took a step. His shoes no longer blinked. "Did you guys see that?!" he said. "Those dumb bugs just sucked the power from my light-up shoes!"

Alexander's eyes widened. "That must be why my clock and the pencil sharpeners and the stoplights all stopped working! I bet these zapper-bugs have been sucking power out of *everything*!" he said.

"And that's why the escalators and lights have been wonky, too," Nikki added.

Alexander looked around. Huge cables ran along the rooftop. They were connected to a giant metal box.

"This dial must be what Ms. Vanderpants was talking about with that electrician," he said. "The school's power is down to zero!"

HUMMMMMMM!

"Look!" said Nikki. She pointed to a nearby antenna tower. All the humming zapper-bugs zoomed up, up, up. A giant, glowing, green roundish-thing hung from the top of the tower. Arcs of lightning shot out from the pod.

"So *that's* where the crazy green lightning's coming from," said Rip.

The zapper-bugs zipped around the pod, humming and flashing. One-by-one, they landed on the pod, and — **BLORP!** They were all absorbed into it.

"What *is* that thing?" asked Rip.

"It's a cocoon!" said Nikki.

"Man, oh, man," said Rip. "The moth inside must be gigantic!"

FWOOM!

The cocoon blasted open with an explosion of sparks.

A nine-foot tall bug monster burst out.

"Who are you calling a moth?" it grunted.

CHAPTER 14 BUG OUT!

The giant bug unfurled its wings. The monster had six legs and a fat, round tail that glowed neon green.

"FINALLY!" said the monster. It had a buzzy voice, as though it were speaking through a kazoo. "My zapper-bugs have charged me up enough to break free from my cocoon!"

Alexander looked at Rip and Nikki. All three of them took a few steps back.

The monster narrowed its bug-eyes. "Where do you think *you're* going? No one escapes THE MIGHTY THUNDERBUG!" The insect clapped its wings together, creating an ear-smashing crash of thunder.

The blast knocked Alexander, Rip, and Nikki down like bowling pins.

KER-BOOOOOOOM!!

"Look at this marvelous electrical system!" said the thunderbug. With three of its legs, the monster pointed to the giant wind fan, the solar panels and the Power Level box.

Alexander sat up. His head was ringing. Rip and Nikki looked dizzy, too.

"Your new school was the perfect place to nest!" the thunderbug continued. "I've drunk up all its power. Even the static electricity from the carpet!"

The monster clapped its hands, making little sparks in the air.

Nikki got to her feet. "But why do you *need* all this power?" she asked. Alexander and Rip stood beside her.

The monster blinked its bug-eyes. "To zap people, of course! You humans swat, smoosh, and zap bugs everyday! But now *I'm* doing the zapping!"

The monster's tail crackled with electricity.

The thunderbug blasted a bolt of green lighting at the S.S.M.P.

KAZZZAP!

15 AMPED UP

R ip Bonkowski was quick, strong, and good at shoving people to the ground. So without thinking, he shoved Alexander and Nikki aside. The charge of lightning exploded onto his chest.

"*Ub-ub-ub-ub-ub!*" Rip shook in place as green sparks traveled up and down his legs.

"RIP!!!" shouted Alexander.

"You're glowing green!" said Nikki.

"Ha!" buzzed the thunderbug. "One pest down, two to go!"

Rip took a wobbly step. "I'm okay. My arms and legs just feel numb — like they fell asleep! *WHOAA!*" His knees buckled and he fell onto a toolbox. Wrenches and hammers spilled out.

BWA-HAHA!

The thunderbug's laugh sounded like a chainsaw. The monster leaned over Rip, poking him in the arm. "My zap has totally numbed you. Now lie still, while I zap your little friends. Then I will swat all three of you with my THUNDERCLAP WINGS!"

The monster looked up. "Who's next?!"

Alexander and Nikki stood on either side of the thunderbug. Alexander saw Nikki reach down to pick up one of the spilled wrenches. It was huge — the size of a baseball bat. She smiled.

"I'm next!" said Alexander. "If you can catch me!" He jumped over some cables and crouched behind the Power Level box.

POWER LEVEL

0%

"Oh, please!" said the thunderbug. "You can't outrun me! I'm lightning-fast!"

The monster fired another lightning bolt at Alexander. He ducked. The bolt hit the Power Level box, showering the roof with sparks. Alexander watched the Power Level dial move up from 0% to 5%.

Alexander gasped. *That blast gave power* back *to the school!*

"Drat, I missed!" said the thunderbug. "Next time I'll —"

WHONK! Nikki had jumped out from behind an air duct. She swung the wrench at the thunderbug's sparkling tail.

"Nice swing, Nikki!" Rip shouted from down on the ground.

But Nikki was shaking in place, saying, *"Ub-ub-ub-ub-ub!"* Green sparks surged from the monster's tail, traveled up the wrench, and danced all over her glowing, green body.

Rip gasped.

Nikki fell over. Her wrench clattered to the ground near Alexander's feet.

"Steee-rike two!" said the thunderbug. "Silly humans! Lightning flows *through* metal!"

The creature turned to face Alexander. It rubbed its wings together, making tiny crackles of electricity. Alexander felt the hairs prickle on the back of his neck.

Rip and Nikki lay sprawled on the rooftop like dropped action figures. The thunderbug stepped over them, moving closer to Alexander.

"Run, Salamander!" cried Nikki.

"Don't let it zap you!" shouted Rip.

But Alexander didn't run. He reached for the wrench. The thunderbug grinned.

"Go ahead—grab it!" said the monster. "You'd be giving me an easy target! I'll zap that wrench, and BLAMMO!"

Zap the wrench?! thought Alexander. *That's it! I know just what to do!*

"Since you're the last pest standing," said the thunderbug, opening its wings, "I'm going to give you a *super*charge!"

"READY?" The monster rubbed its antennae together.

Alexander yanked Dr. Tallow's rubber gloves from his backpack.

"AIM!" The thunderbug yelled. Its tail sizzled.

Alexander snapped the gloves on and picked up the wrench.

"FIRE!" The thunderbug blasted a super-bolt of lightning at the wrench.

The bolt hit one end of the wrench, just as Alexander jammed the other end into the Power Level box.

The Power Level dial cracked as it shot up to 20,000%. The wrench had become a lightning rod, drawing the electricity into the box.

"I'VE BEEN OVERPOWERED!" screamed the thunderbug. The monster vibrated in place. Then it burst into a million sparks. The sparks fizzled away like tiny fireworks.

"Way to go, Salamander!" said Rip, sitting up. "Hey — I can feel my legs again!"

Nikki flopped over onto her elbows. "*Wowee!* Look at the power level!" she said. "Our school will have enough electricity for 500 years!"

"Yeah," said Rip. "I just wish my new shoes still lit up."

Alexander peeled off his gloves, and took out the notebook. Then he plopped down near his friends. "Great teamwork, guys," he said, holding his hands out for a double-fist bump.

Rip, Nikki, and Alexander knocked knuckles.

"*Yow!*" said Alexander. "Another shocking victory for the S.S.M.P.!"

Rip and Nikki rolled their eyes.

Alexander smiled, and took out a pencil to add another monster to the notebook.

THUNDERBUG

Power-hungry giant insect that shoots electricity

HABITAT Cocoon near a power source.

DIET Electricity stolen from alarm clocks, escalators, batteries, etc.

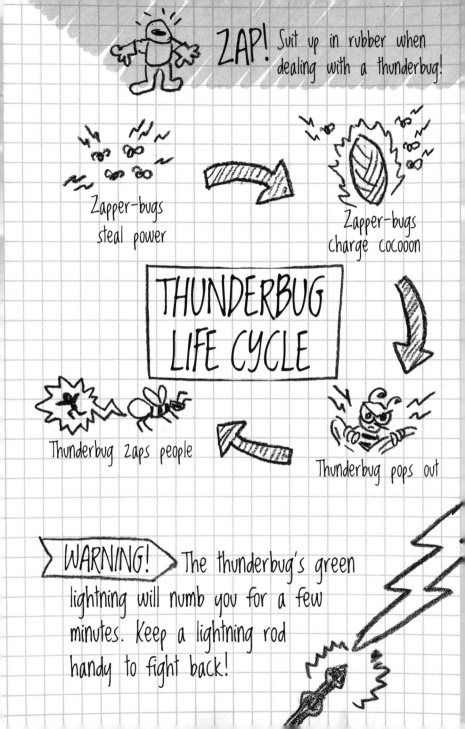

TROY CUMMINGS

has no tail, no wings, no fangs, no claws, and only one head. As a kid, he believed that monsters might really exist. Today, he's sure of it.

 **BEHAVIOR** When this creature is not writing or drawing, he is watching old cartoons from the 1950s.

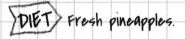 **HABITAT** Troy Cummings likes to read on his sparkly couch.

DIET Fresh pineapples.

EVIDENCE Few people believe that Troy Cummings is real. The only proof we have is that he supposedly wrote and illustrated The Eensy-Weensy Spider Freaks Out!, and Giddy-up, Daddy!

WARNING! Keep your eyes peeled for more danger in The Notebook of Doom #9:

RUMBLE OF THE COASTER GHOST

THE NOTEBOOK OF DOOM

QUESTIONS & ACTIVITIES!

Name some clues that show something weird is happening in Stermont.

Al *raced*, *dashed*, and *scooted* to get to school as fast as possible. Think of words with similar meanings that could describe his trip to school. Use the dictionary or thesaurus for help!

Look at the picture on page 17. How is the new Stermont Elementary building the **same** and **different** from your school?

How does Rip's fashion choice help the students escape the planetarium?

Reread pages 5-6, 34-35, and 48-49. Then choose a monster: trash-squatch, manta x-ray, or rust-buster. Explain your choice and write about how you would defeat it.